HAUNTS & HAM SANDWICHES

CHRISTIAN COZY MYSTERY

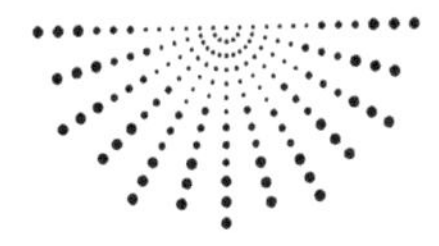

DONNA DOYLE

PUREREAD.COM

CONTENTS

1
THE COST OF VOLUNTEERING

"Sammy, dear, are you ever going to stop smiling?" Helen asked as she poured herself a mug of coffee to start the day.

"I can if you really want me to," Sammy returned with a grin. "No, I take that back. I don't think I can. If I tried too hard, I might just explode." Even as she said it, she almost started laughing.

Her boss shook her head, but she was smiling too. "You know, when I hired you it was solely because of your baking skills. You haven't disappointed me there, but I had no idea you'd be so good for PR. If there's anyone in this town who didn't know you before, they certainly do now."

"I didn't do it to get any attention." The mayor of Stone Springs, Stephen Montgomery, had recently come to Sunny Cove as part of his campaign trail for governor. Since he was such an advocate for the homeless, Sammy and Rob Hewitt had volunteered to help organize the events. It turned into a much bigger ordeal than they ever could've imagined, but it ended with a generous donation from the retired actor.

"Oh, I know that, dear. But if you're as determined to do something to help the homeless as I think you are, then media attention is only going to help you. Don't forget your face was on TV right next to Mr. Montgomery. You've been working really hard to bring this attention to light, and I think it's paid off. It's not bad for business, either." Helen sipped her coffee as she stalked to the front door and flipped over the sign. Some of the regulars were already on their way to the door, ready for their coffee and freshly baked breakfast treats from Sammy.

"True enough." Sammy loved working on local civic issues. She'd already helped start Sunny Cove Services, which helped disabled adults find meaningful work. It proved to be much harder to find a way to get men and women off the streets and into warm beds, but she was resolved to make it happen.

"By the way, I'm going to use my first break to meet with Andrew Herzog. Actually, he's coming here. I figured it would take less time, and I've taken far too much time off work lately."

Helen scoffed. "I'll bet he is coming here! The little rat heard about that donation from Mr. Montgomery, and he's eager to get his hands on it."

Sammy knew that was probably true. The land developer was always driven by money. Sammy hadn't even had to seek him out to get an estimate for the homeless shelter she wanted to build. He came and found her. "I know he's caused a little bit of excitement in town here and there," she hedged, "but there's no harm in listening to what he has to say. Maybe he's got something really good this time."

"You don't think he's just going to try to sell you that same plan he tried to sell me for a new restaurant? And every other business that needed a new building in the last couple of years?" Helen poured a cup of coffee for a local truck driver and headed into the kitchen to fetch the man a cinnamon roll.

"It's possible. We'll see." Sammy had already thought of that, and as she began taking orders she thought of it again. She liked to think that Andrew might've changed a bit, now that he was married to Jamie

Stewart and had the chance to settle down and perhaps start a family. She'd find out soon enough.

She let herself get lost in providing platters of biscuits and gravy, eggs and biscuits. Sammy enjoyed the susurrus of the restaurant when it was busy, the way that voices and plates and chairs all combined together to create a soothing tone that let her know just how well Just Like Grandma's was doing. She'd been working hard since she'd come home to Sunny Cove and found a job with Helen that allowed her to start her life over again after the divorce. While she knew she was under no contractual obligation to make sure business stayed booming for the older woman, it always made her feel good to know the doors wouldn't be closing any time soon.

When Andrew Herzog entered a few hours later, Sammy felt her heart leap up into her throat. She was so excited about hearing what he had to say that it was making her nervous. "Just have a seat right over there," she directed, pointing at a small table in the back that was less than ideal for customers but perfect for a private business chat. "I'll be with you in a second."

"Watch your back," Helen whispered as Sammy came around behind the counter to put the coffee pot down.

"I can handle myself," she returned with a smile.

When she'd taken off her apron, Sammy joined Mr. Herzog at the table. "I'm eager to see what you've got for me. I know I'm no architect or designer, but I've had a few ideas about what might work. I've been trying to find a solution for these poor people for several months, and I've even been looking at the designs of other shelters around the country."

"So have I!" Andrew enthused. He was an extremely tall man who didn't fit quite right on the dining chair. Dressed impeccably from his designer suit to his carefully combed hair, he was always trying to be as professional as possible. "I've been spending a lot of time on this design."

Sammy brightened a little, taking this as a sign that he wasn't just up to his same old tricks. "Wonderful! Let's see it!"

Andrew opened a laptop and turned it around, showing her the design on the screen. "What we're looking at is a fairly large building, because you want to be able to house as many people as possible. But I did take into account the fact that you'd also want to use space wisely. I not only looked at homeless shelter designs but the new styles of micro-apartments that are taking over in big cities like New York and Hong Kong."

Intrigued, Sammy leaned forward to study the screen as he continued his virtual tour. "When guests—because I think that's a nicer thing to call them—come in the front door, they'll be greeted in a reception room. It's very simplified, where they can punch all their information in on a touchscreen that will automatically assign them a room number based on how many people are in their party. For instance, there would be a differently designed room for a family than for a single person."

Sammy was already feeling a little overwhelmed. "A touchscreen? I mean, that's really nice, but I think I'd rather have someone there at the front desk who can make them feel welcome."

"But the computer already keeps track of who is in what room and what availabilities there are, plus you don't have to pay it a wage or find a volunteer. And the computer will automatically reassign the key codes for the electronic locks." He spoke as though this was all perfectly common knowledge.

"Wait, what? Electronic locks?"

Herzog nodded. "Absolutely! My research shows that people don't always seek help from shelters because they feel they are dangerous. All those people in one big room, coming from all walks of life. I can understand that feeling. But each room will have an electronic lock, and the code—as I said —will be changed for each occupant. Guests will feel safe and secure in their individual rooms."

"Okay." Sammy could see the validity of this, but she was already adding up the costs of those locks. "Go on."

"This is where it gets really exciting." Herzog switched the screen to show what looked like several layouts of the same apartment. "The best feature of these little places is the furniture. Just a few basic pieces convert easily from a couch to a bed to a dining table. There's lots of storage space in the built-in cabinets, a small but serviceable kitchen, and accordion walls that can separate the room for additional privacy when needed."

Sammy frowned. "That all sounds amazing, but wouldn't it make more sense to provide a large kitchen in a common area? These people really just need a place to wash up and sleep, and everything else can happen downstairs."

"But Sammy, you need the guests to be as self-sufficient as possible. I know I've heard Rob voice some concerns about how you're going to continue the funding of this place once the donation money from Mr. Montgomery is gone, and you'll have enough to deal with just in maintenance and taxes."

Yes, that was true, especially if any of the fancy stuff he wanted to put into the shelter broke down. But he did have a point about not needing a bunch of staff to run the place. "I'll have to think about it, and of course discuss it with Rob. Do you have a bid sheet?"

"Of course." Herzog produced a high-quality printout from a folder and handed it over.

Sammy took the thick sheet of paper. Her eyes immediately skimmed past the breakdown of all the locks and computers and furniture to find the bottom line, and her stomach sank down into her shoes. "Wow."

"Don't forget that modern living always comes at a price," Andrew said. "It seems like a lot right now, I know, but over time I think you'll be really happy."

Taking a deep breath, Sammy blew it out through her lips. The hefty price tag didn't even include the property they'd need to build the shelter on, and it was already blowing their budget out of the water. "I think I'll have to explore some other options."

He patted the bid sheet. "Don't make any decisions today. You need time to figure out what's best, and I get that. But don't be too hasty with any of it."

"Right. Well, thanks for meeting me here. I'd better get back to work." When she'd seen him out the door with a complimentary doughnut, Sammy pressed her hand to her forehead in concern.

"Didn't go so well?" Helen asked, looking superior.

"Check this out." Sammy handed over the proposal and told her what Herzog had designed. "It's a really neat idea, and I think it could work out if we lived in a different city and had more funding. There's just no way we can build something like this."

Helen studied the figures, tipping her head to the side and tapping her chin. "Why don't you explore what it would cost to fix up an existing building? It might not be all high-tech and fancy, but you might find a really good deal."

"That's a good idea." And it was such a good idea that Sammy wondered why she hadn't thought about it before. She was already starting to get excited again.

2

A GHOST OF ITS FORMER SELF

"This is a classic Victorian structure in the Second Empire style, as noted by the distinct mansard roof and the tower." Edith Margrave gestured to the massive house. "The round dormer window in the cupola is particularly unusual and makes it a stunning feature of the house."

"Wow." Sammy tipped her head back as she examined the massive house, which seemed to reach all the way up to the sky. Sure, there were much bigger structures in larger cities, but for a small town like Sunny Cove this was massive. The house was three stories tall, four if you counted the tower.

"Wow, indeed," Edith said with an appreciative nod. "Also note the decorative window surrounds and the cornices. You won't find architectural details like that on any of the more modern homes you might see around here."

The window surrounds were indeed very pretty, but most of them surrounded pieces of plywood instead of actual windows. The peeling yellow paint—at least, Sammy was fairly certain it had once been yellow—didn't do the place any favors, and neither did the overgrown yard. Granted, spring hadn't hit full force so there wasn't much greenery around, but the spindly traces of ivy that crept up the wooden siding contributed to the creepy look of the house.

"I think I remember this place from when I was a kid. An old woman lived here, and nobody wanted to come by to trick-or-treat because they were afraid of her. I think there were some other stories along those lines, too, but I can't remember." She'd have to ask Heather later.

The realtor tsked. "Kids are silly, and people like to spread rumors like that just to scare themselves." She stepped up into the entryway and unlocked the front door. "And of course, nobody lives here anymore, so that only makes the rumors fly faster."

"How long has it been unoccupied?" A musty smell emanated from the house before Sammy had even walked inside, but that was to be expected.

"Oh, quite some time to be honest with you. But I've had several other folks interested in the place, and I expect one couple to put a bid in anytime. How long have you been interested in fixing up historical houses?"

Sammy followed Edith into the wide entryway. A set of wooden stairs that had probably been beautiful at one point in time led up to the second story. Peeling wallpaper hung from the walls like limp ghosts. Wide doorways on either side led to other rooms, but Sammy couldn't see much into the rooms because of the boarded up windows. "Only recently. I'm looking for something I can fix up and turn into a homeless shelter."

Edith's eyes widened. "Oh. You know, I might have a place that will work a little better for you on the other side of town. It was an apartment building. It does need a lot of work, but it's much newer than this one. You won't have as much to do to bring the electrical and plumbing all up to code, plus you won't need to worry about preserving all the historic, architectural details."

"We can take a look at that, but a friend recommended this place to me." Kate had driven by and seen the For-Sale sign, and it sounded too good to resist at least looking at. There was something exciting about walking through an old home, especially one that had over a hundred years of history behind it.

Sammy stepped through one of the big doorways and found herself in a room that must have been some sort of parlor. She had to use the flashlight feature on her phone to see anything in the dark space. Although someone had covered the floor in hideous orange shag carpeting and the decorative trim that had probably once been in here was removed, she could really see the potential for a common area. Edith stalked behind her as she explored the first floor and marveled at the size of the rooms.

"Mind if we look upstairs?" she asked as they returned to the foyer. She put one foot on the first step, hoping the staircase was up to the task.

The realtor shrugged. "Feel free, but I injured my knee last week and I can't climb all those stairs. This staircase runs all the way up to the third floor, where that mansard roof I mentioned allows for a full top story. There's a separate staircase to access the top floor of the tower, but I can't make any guarantees as to what shape it's in."

Sammy understood the risk, but she was too excited to care. She could feel a ball of exhilaration building in the pit of her stomach at the thought of this new adventure, and there was nothing she wanted more than to dive into it and get it done. She would do the logical thing and look at the apartment building Edith wanted to show her, as well as any other houses in the area that might work, but Sammy already had a feeling this was going to be *the* place.

The rooms on the second floor were large, and she was surprised to find that they each had closets. "I thought old houses didn't have closets," she marveled as she remembered hearing stories about how they just used wardrobes instead. There was only one bathroom on this floor to be shared among four bedrooms and a study, and it looked desperate for a remodel.

The third floor was as the realtor had described it. From the outside of the building, it was practically hidden by the squared off roof and yet was just as spacious as the rest of the house. Half the floor was simply a wide attic space, but it could easily be partitioned into sleeping quarters.

At the end of the upper hall, Sammy experimentally opened a door. On the floor below, this area had been a study. Here it was the entrance to the tower that Edith had promised. A small empty room simply held a rickety looking staircase that clung to the wall. Craning her head upward, Sammy could trace it to the final, highest point of the house, but she couldn't be sure that the ancient boards would bear her weight.

She was just about to try it when a loud noise sounded from the other end of the house. Sammy jumped, letting go of the unsteady handrail and running for the door. She burst into the hall, panting and looking around. The door that led to the attic space was standing open, shuddering on its hinges. Cautiously, Sammy crept around the banister and poked her head in the room, wondering if the realtor had managed to follow her all the way up here. The space was empty, but she noticed the window on the other end was open and a fine spring breeze was blowing in.

Sammy laughed, and then she laughed a little harder at herself. It was an old house, and she had let a cracked window scare her into believing the rumors for a minute. But Sammy didn't believe in ghosts except for the Holy Ghost, and there was nothing in this house to be afraid of except for all the dust, dirt, and broken-down furniture that had been left inside it. The shag carpeting that prevailed throughout the house was something to be intimidated by, as well.

Heading back downstairs, Sammy thought she was ready to leave. She'd kept Edith waiting long enough. But she couldn't help having one last peek through the rooms as she imagined what these spaces could mean for someone who had no home. Sure, it was rough right now. There was no way they could afford to restore it to the former beauty of its heyday, but a few efficient LED lights and some easy-to-clean flooring and it could be amazing.

She poked her head into the study, taking in the old oak desk and a few books that were scattered on the floor. Sammy gingerly picked one up, seeing that it was actually a hardback journal. It was difficult to read the faded, scrawling hand, but Sammy soon made out that she was looking at a recipe book. Her heart lurched with eagerness, but she had to remember that it wasn't hers. She hadn't bought the house yet, after all. Sammy gingerly put the book in the center of the desk and practically skipped down the stairs.

3

NOT ALONE

"I'm surprised Edith gave you the key," Sammy commented as she watched Rob unlock the door to the house. "She seemed like the type who'd be a stickler for the rules. I don't think she liked me looking at the house on my own, but she didn't have a choice with that injured knee."

He raised one blonde eyebrow. "Her knee seemed perfectly fine to me, but I wasn't exactly looking. And I've worked with her on a few things in the past, so she knows me. You sure about this place?" He glanced overhead, where spider webs and bits of debris had gathered around the light fixture by the front door.

"The contractor will really help determine that. I figured it was smart to have him come out and give us a bid so we will really know if we can afford this place plus the repairs. But come look in here! You can tell it was once an absolutely beautiful home. I'd love to find some pictures of what it looked like when everything was all original. It was her second time being in the house, and now she could see more of the potential of the house instead of the coat of grime that covered everything.

Rob followed her around. "Big rooms. The kitchen would need a lot of work, but we should be able to get prefabricated cabinets fairly cheap. If the contractor thinks he can make it work, then we'll need to get an inspector out here to find any problems we can't see."

"Like ghosts?" she joked, thinking of that slamming door.

The lawyer opened a door in the kitchen, revealing a set of stairs that led down to a basement. "Like foundation problems or electrical work that could be dangerous."

"I didn't even see the basement!" Sammy exclaimed, hardly hearing him. "Let's explore it!"

But a knock on the front door stopped them, and they returned to the entryway to admit Ken Lowry. He'd done a small amount of work on the Sunny

Cove Services building for them, and he carried an old-fashioned wooden toolbox in one hand. Tall and slim with a head of thick brown hair that had a mind of its own, he stepped across the threshold nervously. "Hey, Sammy, Rob. You sure this is the right place? It doesn't look like a homeless shelter to me."

"I know," Sammy admitted, hoping that soon enough she could get others to see the vision that was quickly building inside her head. "But I think it could be."

Ken scratched his ear. "Let's take a walk through. I'll take some measurements and you can tell me what kind of ideas you have. Keep in mind that a house this old is going to have more problems than you think. A small project will probably be much bigger than you imagine."

"Maybe so, but even if we have to do it in sections it'll be better than those poor people sleeping by the dumpster behind the department store." Sammy escorted him and Rob through the main rooms of the house, once again going over her vision. The contractor had his measuring tape and a notebook at the ready, and he took notes almost constantly.

He paused when they reached the second story. "You know, I'm surprised you'd even consider this house."

Sammy sighed. "Look, I know it's in really bad shape, but I'm willing to do a lot of work myself."

"It's not that." Ken perched his pencil on top of his ear as he squinted up the staircase that led to the next floor. "It's the fact that everyone in town thinks it's haunted."

"I've heard people say that," Rob replied, "but we all know there's no such thing as ghosts. The house has been vacant, plus it's big and imposing. The way it looks right now, it might as well be a haunted house from a Halloween movie."

"And this is a great opportunity to change that and improve the way our town looks," Sammy pointed out, realizing that this project could be even more of a community service project than she'd initially realized.

The contractor sighed as he took a few cautious steps toward one of the bedroom doors and looked inside. "Yeah, and that's all grand. But do you think it's very fair to make a place for homeless people and then expect them to sleep in the same room as some ghosts?" He watched the upper corners of the walls as though he expected a misty white apparition to show up.

Sammy pursed her lips. She hadn't thought about it like that before. Even though she didn't believe there were any spirits here, that didn't mean other people would feel the same way. "Well, I can see what you mean. But I think if we fix the house up, it'll change what people think. A bright, pretty house is going to feel a lot different than an old decrepit one."

"I guess that's true. Did you hear that?" Ken stiffened, his heavy brows creasing.

Sammy folded her hands in front of her chest. "Very funny."

"No, I'm serious. I just heard a strange noise." Ken crept down the hall, pausing at each doorway.

Sammy looked at Rob, who shrugged. "I didn't hear anything."

They followed Ken, who'd entered the last bedroom at the end of the hall. He was standing in the middle of the floor. In here, the crusty shag carpeting was an odd green color. A saggy mattress leaned against one wall. He had a look of concentration on his face as he continued to listen. "There it is again!"

This time, Sammy heard it. The sound was a scrabbling noise, like there was something trapped in the wall. She was trying hard to be practical about this, but her mind instantly traveled to spooky stories she'd heard at camp as a kid. The hairs on the back of her neck stood up, and she held onto her own arms to keep from shivering.

"Over here." Ken headed for the corner of the room, pointing upward at the ceiling. The noise sounded again, a scratching from the other side of the peeling wallpaper.

"Maybe it's something on the third floor?" Rob mused, staring at the spot in the wall as they all were.

The contractor leapt on that idea, jogging out of the room and around the stairs to climb to the next level. Sammy followed the two men, intrigued to find out what this was all about but worried they might find something more than they bargained for.

Ken headed to the attic space, which was right above the bedroom where they'd been standing only a moment ago. He walked along the wall until he heard the sound again, and this time it was accompanied by a high-pitched trill. The contractor started laughing.

"What is it?" Sammy had never heard such a noise in her life, and while she continued to tell herself she didn't believe in ghosts, the experience was a little too weird.

Ken, however, was no longer worried about what the odd noise might be. He was peeling back the wood paneling that covered one wall, sending splinters and dust down to the floor.

"Um, you might not want to do that," Rob advised.

But Ken didn't listen. He pulled back another section of paneling and reached into the wall. When he pulled his hand back out, it was holding a small furry body. "It's a baby raccoon!"

Sammy's heart melted. "Oh, the poor thing! How did it get in there?" She reached out a finger to touch the top of the baby's head. It watched her through its mask with wide eyes as it continued the trilling noises it made while in the wall.

"Probably the mama crawled in through a hole in the roof somewhere and made a nest. When the baby got old enough to start wandering around, it fell down in here. I don't see the other babies or the mama, so that's my best guess. Plus, I've seen it happen in other houses as well."

"What do we do with it?" Rob was petting the little furball now, too, and he looked just as enchanted with it as Sammy felt. "I can probably find the number for the local wildlife rescue."

"No need." The contractor tucked the little critter up under his chin, where it burrowed against his neck and chittered happily. "Mama's probably out looking for him. We can put him outside, and she'll come get him as soon as we're gone." He headed for the stairs, cradling the creature and chuckling to himself. "Can't believe I let myself get spooked like that."

Sammy could believe it, because she'd allowed herself to do the same thing. It was laughable now, but it hadn't been in the moment. She felt terrible for the poor little raccoon and hoped its mother would find it as Ken promised.

They found an old cardboard box and set it on its side on the porch so the little animal would have some shelter while it waited and they headed to their cars.

"Is there anything else you need from us?" Rob asked.

"No, I should be good to go. I'll just need to draw up a few things and put some figures together, and I'll call you in a few days. Oh, and if the owners get mad at me for damaging that wall, you can just tell them I'll fix it for free. Not that a little bit of broken paneling makes much difference here, but it was worth it to save that little guy." He got in his truck and drove away, still laughing.

Sammy leaned against her car and sighed as she looked up at the house. "Do you think Ken was right about inviting homeless people into a house that's reportedly haunted? Will that make them stay away? I mean, it would be a shame to go to all the expense and effort only to have everyone too scared to make use of it."

Rob joined her in studying the house. "You know, when I see an old place like this, I always imagine what people must've said about it when it was first built. It wouldn't have looked haunted or spooky to them. It would have been the height of style and architecture, the envy of everyone in the neighborhood. We are raised to think that old stuff is the same as scary stuff."

"That's a good point." Sammy had never imagined that touring a house for sale would make her think so much about the vulnerability of the human mind, and especially her own. It was too easy to put ideas into people's heads. "Well, I better get going. I need to go put some time in at the restaurant."

"Helen sure is nice to let you take so much time off," Rob commented. "I guess all those cakes and pies are worth it for her."

Sammy nodded, feeling guilty. "She's been extremely understanding, and I know I'd never get that kind of treatment anywhere else. I'm really grateful to her."

"I think she understands what you're doing for this town. Helen has lived in Sunny Cove all her life, and it's important to her."

"Don't say it's what ***I'm*** doing for this town," Sammy corrected. "You've played a very important role yourself, as well as all the other people who've come together to make things happen. It's all part of God's plan, not mine."

Rob winked. "Maybe, but I think you've at least got a little something to do with it. Call me when you hear from the contractor, and we'll go from there."

"Will do." Sammy got in her car, and Rob waited until she had the engine running before he pulled out of the driveway. She went back to Just Like Grandma's, where she baked up a storm and wondered what life must've been like for those who lived in the big beautiful house when it was brand new. She hoped she'd have a chance to ask Edith about the recipe book in the study and whether she could maybe at least have a chance to buy that journal. There was no telling what sort of interesting dishes it contained.

Later that night, when her feet ached from being on them all day and she finally returned home, Sammy got a text from Ken Lowry. She was excited to open it and see what he had to say, but it didn't actually have anything to do with the bid for the house.

Went by the house; just had to check. Mama raccoon has retrieved her baby.

Sammy smiled. At least that was one thing taken care of.

4

RUMOR HAS IT

Sammy hummed to herself at work the next day. She'd had dreams all night of that beautiful house and what it would look like if someone just scraped off all the old paint and put on a new coat. They could go with the yellow that'd been on there most recently, or they could do something completely different. A deep blue would make a nice contrast with white trim. Or maybe a pale green? It was hard to decide, but she knew the paint color was really the last choice she needed to worry about.

"Uh oh. You've got that look on your face again," Kate said with a smile as she came in the kitchen for an order.

"What look is that?" Sammy asked innocently.

"Oh, you know. The one that says you're working on something. You get that dreamy, distant look in your eyes, but you still have your brows drawn down and your jaw tight like you're concentrating really hard."

Sammy had to laugh at that, and she rubbed her hands down her cheeks to wipe away the expression Kate had pointed out. "I didn't even know I did that!"

"You do! But I don't mind, because I know it means you have something interesting to say. Tell me all about it." Kate, having worked at Just Like Grandma's for a while now, expertly whipped up four plates of biscuits and gravy. It was a staple at the restaurant that was served at all hours, so a big pan of warm biscuits and a vat of gravy were always available.

"Okay, but only if you let me help you carry those." Sammy grabbed two of the plates and followed Kate into the dining room. Business had hit a mid-morning lull between the breakfast rush and the lunchtime scrabble, and it was nice that things were a bit quiet. They deposited the plates at the appropriate table and returned to the counter for some coffee.

"Kate, I can't tell you how glad I am that you noticed that house for sale. It's absolutely gorgeous, or at least it has the potential to be."

Kate clapped her hands in excitement. "That's great! I know it looks like a bit of a haunted house right now, but if there's anyone who can turn it around, it's you."

"It's funny you should say that." Sammy filled her in on the slamming door, Ken Lowry's uncertainty about the house and the naughty raccoon. "I mean, I know it's not haunted. But now that everyone else is telling me that, my imagination keeps running away with me. Well, that is until I start thinking about house plans again."

The two of them laughed as they discussed the possibilities for adding bathrooms, splitting larger rooms in half to make more private spaces, and how the intake process might work. "Andrew Herzog had some wonderful ideas for a really high-end place, but I think it belongs in an episode of *The Jetsons* instead of Sunny Cove."

Kate made a dismissive noise. "We all know how he is. If you showed him that house, he'd have a bulldozer out there in about two seconds."

"That's probably true." Sammy looked to the front door when she heard the little bell over it ring. It admitted an older woman with long curly hair down to her waist. She wore tiny wireframe glasses and a loose sweater over a long dress. She looked to Sammy like the kind of person who'd teach poetry to college students.

"Welcome to Just Like Grandma's!" she called out. "Feel free to have a seat anywhere."

But the woman strode forward confidently in her suede boots, and Sammy first noticed the stack of folders under her arm. "I'm not here to have a meal. I'm looking for Sammy Baker."

"I am she."

The woman nodded her gray head as if she'd already known this. "My name is Noreen Heinz. I'm on the executive board of the Sunny Cove Historical Society. I understand that you're interested in purchasing a house on Liberty Street?" The severity of the woman's dark blue eyes as she looked over her glasses at Sammy was intimidating.

"Well, yes. I mean, I'm considering it. I have to wait on some figures to come back to see what—"

"And I understand you're planning to turn the building into a shelter of some sort?"

"That's the plan. You see, there are a lot more homeless people in Sunny Cove than most folks realize, and I've been trying to find a way to truly help them. We recently got a very generous donation from—"

But Ms. Heinz wasn't interested in hearing any of that, and she didn't seem to care one way or another what happened to the homeless or how Sammy had gotten the money to help them. "You see, Ms. Baker, the age of the house means that it might have some historical and architectural significance. It's one of the oldest houses in Sunny Cove, and as such it's my duty to see whether or not it belongs on the preservation list."

All the thrill that had been building up inside Sammy since she'd first gone to look at the house was in imminent danger of fizzling out. "The preservation list?"

"Yes, of course. Surely, you've heard that there are some homes the Historical Society has worked to help preserve in their original state. There's a lot we can learn from these homes, and even though most of them are privately owned, both the local and national Historical Societies have a vested interest in making sure they're treated properly."

Sammy swallowed. "What do you need to do?"

"The process is very simple. I'll walk through the house and take a lot of pictures and notes. I'll need you present for this, because I'll also need to know what your plans are for the house. For instance, if there's an original fireplace that dates back to 1885 when the house was built, then I can't let you rip it out in favor of a more modern aesthetic."

"I see." And Sammy did, but she wasn't sure she liked it. "And what happens if the house *does* need to be put on the preservation list?"

Ms. Heinz shrugged with one shoulder, as though the answer was plain and simple. "Then every step of the remodeling process must be run by the Historical Society and approved. Here's my card." She produced a business card from the stack of folders she'd brought in with her. "If you could please arrange a time to for the walkthrough, just give me a call and I'll be there."

Sammy accepted it, feeling dumbfounded as she watched the woman turn on her heel and walk back out the door. "Did that really just happen?"

Kate leaned her elbows heavily on the counter. "It sure did. What are you going to do?"

Looking down at the business card in her hand, Sammy slipped it in her pocket. "The only thing I can do right now is go with her for the walkthrough. I'll tell her everything I want to do. Then she'll turn around and tell me that some ancient light switch is more important than housing the homeless, and I'll be back at square one." She sighed as she joined Kate in leaning on the counter, wishing she had an old rag to throw down to really show just how defeated she felt.

"It might not be that bad," Kate said hopefully.

"No, but sometimes I think getting this project done is like beating my head against a brick wall. I run into an obstacle every time I turn around. It's getting difficult." She just wanted to do some good for the community. The money from Mr. Montgomery had seemed like the ray of sunshine they were waiting for, but clearly there was more that needed to fall into place.

"Hey." Kate put a comforting hand on her arm. "You don't know that this is an obstacle yet. This woman hasn't seen the inside of the house yet, and you did say it was in really bad condition. Maybe it'll be fine. Or you'll just have to preserve that one light switch and you can do what you want everywhere else. Maybe build a little protective box around it. You know, with a display light and a little plaque."

Sammy laughed at that, which was just what Kate had intended, and it felt good. "Yeah, you're right. I can't be a defeatist about this when I don't even know where it's going. And I guess if this house doesn't work out, then it's just not meant to be. It's God's way of telling me something."

"There you go." Kate straightened as a group of five entered the restaurant. "Looks like the start of the lunch rush. You ready?"

"Always." That first group was, as Kate had predicted, just the beginning. Sammy joined her in making sure everyone got seated, their drinks were poured, and their orders taken. It was a good thing she'd already done most of her baking in the first part of the morning, because there certainly wasn't time for it now as she carried bowls of soup and trays of sandwiches and hamburgers out to the customers.

And one of those customers was apparently feeling a little particular, because Kate reported to Sammy that the diner at the table in the corner wanted to see her specifically.

"It's not Noreen Heinz again, is it?" she asked without turning around.

"No, you're safe there. It's your white knight."

Curious what she meant, Sammy glanced behind her to see Sheriff Jones seated with a steaming cup of coffee. She slapped Kate playfully on the arm. "Oh, stop!"

Kate lifted her hands innocently. "Just calling it like I see it. Now go see what he wants, and I'll get this other gentleman his third slice of cherry pie." Kate headed for the bakery counter.

"Is Kate not a good enough waitress for you, is there some sort of secret police business we need to talk about?" Sammy teased as she walked up to the lawman.

He gestured at the chair across from him. "You have a moment?"

Sammy looked around. Just Like Grandma's was well in hand for the moment. "Just a few. I don't want to leave her to this all by herself."

"I understand. I'll make it quick." He waited until she'd sat down before he continued. "I heard a rumor that you're thinking about buying that old Victorian on Liberty Street."

"Not you, too," Sammy groaned.

"What's the matter? Is this supposed to be some secret you and Rob are working on?" His voice was teasing, but Sammy could swear she saw some genuine curiosity—or maybe jealousy?—in his eyes.

Sammy sighed. "It's not a secret, but it's turning out to be a much bigger deal than I thought. I wasn't going to tell many people about it until we knew whether or not it would actually work."

"What's the problem with it?"

Though she had a feeling he already knew, or else he wouldn't be asking, Sammy told him. "First, it seems half this town thinks the house is haunted. I'm not sure how the financials are going to work out, and I can only hope that it's cheaper than building an entirely new structure. Now I've got the Historical Society breathing down my neck, wanting to see if there's anything there worth preserving. If that happens, then I'll just have to find a different place. There's no way we can afford to fix it all up to period, and I don't want to wait for the Society to approve every nail."

"I see." The sheriff nodded and sipped his coffee. "That does sound like quite a problem."

"And I take it you're going to dump another one on my lap? Go ahead and get it over with. I'd rather hear about it sooner than later."

He studied the dark liquid in his mug for a moment. "I'm not at liberty to give you all the details. You know how these things go. But the sheriff's department has received plenty of calls about that neighborhood over the years. Most of it is something silly, like a kid who's gotten himself spooked or a bored housewife who had a little too much sherry. I don't normally think anything of those kinds of calls, and they had dropped off until recently. Now that there's been some activity at the house—namely, you going out there to look at it—things are starting up again."

Sammy felt the weight of the world on her shoulders. "You're saying I've brought attention back to the house, and everyone is convinced all over again that it's haunted. This is just ridiculous."

"I'm not going to argue with you on that. But I know that that old, forgotten house is suddenly front-page news again, and I know you've had some other troubles when it comes to getting this shelter under way. I'm just telling you to be careful, but I don't think it's Casper and his friends that you need to be concerned about."

"Note taken." There was some real logic to what the sheriff had said, even if he was being a bit cryptic about it. "Anything else I need to know?"

He shook his head and drained his coffee. "The only other thing I came here to say was good luck." He winked and pulled change out of his pocket for the drink.

"You know that we don't charge law officers for coffee," Sammy protested. "And that even includes troublesome sheriffs."

"That's all right." He went for the door, leaving Sammy to wonder just what was going to go wrong next.

5
A PIECE OF HISTORY

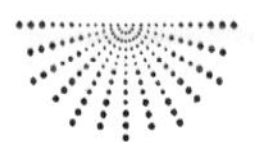

"I know I probably shouldn't be, but I'm nervous," Sammy admitted several days later as she wiped down a table. Just Like Grandma's was about to close for the evening. She should be happy that she was getting off work and that she'd been able to put in plenty of time at the café. Her shelter project had been stalled when Edith had gone on vacation and nobody else at her office seemed able to find the key for the house after Rob had given it back. The realtor was back in town and everything was on track, but it didn't feel like it was.

"What's the worst thing she can do?" Helen asked, grabbing a broom and attacking the floor. It was swept constantly during the day as customers came and went, but the older woman was a stickler for a shining floor.

The same worry Sammy had been having for the past week once again pelted through her mind. "Tell me no. Make me start over."

"So you'll have lost a couple of weeks. It's a very minor setback compared to how long you've been working on this project, and you'll find another place. You're a very talented and committed young lady, and don't you forget it!" Helen had paused with her sweeping to shake her finger at her employee.

Sammy laughed. "This place really is just like Grandma's, complete with the scolding!"

Helen sighed as she moved a chair out of the way to get underneath a table. "The only one I should actually be scolding is myself, to be honest with you."

"What do you mean?" Sammy laid the damp rag on a table and put her hands on her hips, frowning with concern at her boss. "None of this has anything to do with you."

"No, not really. But I should've known Noreen would stick her nose into this." She shook her head as she fetched the dustpan.

Sammy took it from her and bent down, holding the dustpan to the floor so Helen could sweep the collected dirt inside. "You know her?"

"Oh, yes. Noreen and I go way back. We went to school together, actually, but we were never very close. She moved off to the east coast for a bit and came back here when her husband died."

Interesting, but it didn't quite answer Sammy's question. "So what does that have to do with her getting involved in this house?"

Helen pushed through the door into the kitchen to wash her hands. "You know how Andrew Herzog is about wanting to raze all the old buildings and put up new ones? Noreen is basically the complete opposite. She's made it her life's passion to preserve everything from the past she possibly can. I guess that's what she and her late husband did when they lived in the Carolinas, and she wants to continue that here."

"I see." Sammy twisted up her mouth as she took off her apron and checked that everything was ready to go for the next day. "If she hadn't come and visited me, and if she hadn't been so rude about it, I would say that's only a good thing. I mean, it's great when old houses are watched over and protected. I just wish this one wasn't standing in the way of what I want to do."

"I understand, dear." Helen patted her hand. "I'll warn you that Noreen is probably the most aggressive member of the Historical Society. If there's anything in Sunny Cove that has some sort of historical significance, she thinks it belongs in the Smithsonian. Now, don't get me wrong. I think we can all learn a lot from the past, and preservation is important. But we also have to live our lives."

"Let's just hope that Noreen understands at least some of that." Sammy checked her watch. "I've got to go. I'll see you in the morning. Do you want me to say hi to Noreen for you?"

Helen shook her head. "I think you'd stand a better chance if you didn't, dear. Good luck."

Sammy drove slowly down Liberty Street, suddenly paying a lot more attention to the different types of houses in Sunny Cove than she had before. Most of them were bungalows and ranches, some even smaller and simpler. It wasn't like there were massive Victorian houses on every corner. As Sammy drove through, admiring the simplistic houses in a whole new way and wondering just what history they might have, she also wondered what houses *were* on the preservation list. She'd never thought much about the Sunny Cove Historical Society before, and now she was incredibly curious about it. If she and Noreen didn't completely clash with each other, maybe she'd go to their office and find out more.

She slowed down as she neared the house, hugging the curb and trying to look at the house from every angle. She suddenly wanted to know which of the trees were here when the house was new, and how much they'd grown since then. She was curious what kind of plants might've been put in the yard. Did they have a garden? Did the original occupants think their house was fancy, or was it simply run-of-the-mill for them? She might not ever know.

Sammy parked and got out, noting as Mr. Lowry did that the cardboard box where they'd put the baby raccoon was long empty. "I hope your mama found a safer place to put you," she muttered to herself. She couldn't imagine what a woman like Noreen Heinz would think about having wild animals in the wall. Then again, it could work out on Sammy's behalf.

While Sammy waited, she wandered around the property. The two times she'd been to the house, she'd spent all her time indoors. She wanted to see what the rest of the property looked like. The light was swiftly fading, but she could tell that someone had at least been coming by, over the last few years, to run a lawnmower swiftly over the areas that hadn't been completely grown over with bushes and trees. One large maple leaned heavily against the side of the house, and Sammy made a mental note to find out how much it would cost to have it removed. That would be a dangerous thing, and it could be damaging the house as well. She laughed a little to herself when she realized that was probably how the mother racoon had gotten her babies up to the attic.

Around the back, Sammy noticed a particularly bushy area surrounded by a low iron fence. She leaned over it, pulling back some of the overgrown plants. It looked like a garden of some sort, and she was curious just how old it was and what kinds of vegetables someone might've planted here. She couldn't see much, so she lifted one foot to step over the fence.

"I wouldn't do that if I were you," a harsh voice snapped behind her.

Feeling as though she'd just been caught sneaking out of her bedroom late at night, Sammy put her foot back down on the outside of the fence where it belonged. She turned to see Noreen Heinz standing at the corner of the house, looking particularly irritated. "I was just curious what might be in here. I thought—"

"What you probably didn't think was how rude it is to disturb the dead," Noreen corrected.

Sammy glanced over her shoulder at the fence and the tangle of plants. "The dead?"

"I wouldn't doubt it. Plenty of older homes—especially as old as this one—had family burial plots on the grounds. My records show there was a different, smaller house on this same parcel of land before this house was built, so it's likely there are several generations buried back there.

Sammy suddenly felt like she needed a shower. "I had no idea."

"And that, Miss Baker, is exactly why the Historical Society needs people like me. I *do* know, and I'm going to find out every bit of information on this house that I can. That'll probably include the cemetery, but I'll have to come back and go through it when we have more light. For now, we can take a look at the inside of the house, if you'll be so kind as to unlock it." She gestured toward the front of the house with one bony hand.

"Of course." Sammy had considered asking one of her friends to come with her for this walkthrough. Now she was glad nobody was there to see how embarrassing it all was. "The trust that Mr. Hewitt set up for our homeless shelter project went ahead and paid to have the electricity turned on so that it'd be easier to do things like this," Sammy explained, unlocking the door with shaking fingers. She knew most realtors these days used those little lock boxes with codes on them to hide a key, but the antique door handle was probably too delicate. She stepped into the entry hall and began looking for a light switch.

When the overhead fixture suddenly began to shine with a yellowish glow, Sammy sucked in a breath. She hadn't touched the switch.

But Ms. Heinz had her hand on it, and she raised one thick eyebrow. "Are we a little jumpy this evening?"

"I don't mean to be, but everyone else who's been in or even near this house has had something to say about ghosts. You just startled me, that's all."

"My dear, I've been in more old houses than you can possibly imagine. It doesn't bother me at all. Now, let's see what we can find." Noreen immediately turned right into the dining room and found another light switch.

Sammy followed, more interested in how much junk had been left in the place than anything else. She and Rob would need to get a dumpster or two just to get rid of the old furniture, the nasty carpet, and the random assortment of cardboard boxes and things that resided in the house. It would be yet another expense.

"Such a shame," Noreen murmured as she ran her hand down the wall. "You see this here?" She was pointing to a small scrap of paper on the wall that could've been a sticker.

"That was likely part of the original wallpaper. If it was a bigger sample, we could send it off to a place in New York that reproduces antique wallcoverings, upholsteries, and rugs, but I don't think there's enough to get anything out of it." Noreen sniffed, looking thoroughly offended.

"That sounds expensive," Sammy commented.

"Oh, it is, but it's truly worth it. A house really comes alive when you restore it to its former glory. Speaking of, let's see what's under here." Noreen bent down and tugged at a corner of the hideous shag carpeting. "Ah, darn!"

"What is it?" Sammy took a step back, hoping it wasn't cockroaches. She could handle raccoons in the attic, but not cockroaches.

Noreen responded by peeling the carpet further back. "Someone tore out the original hardwood and replaced it with linoleum. Then someone else got tired of that and threw this carpet down. Such a waste. It was probably the same people who removed all the window trim in here. I bet it was beautiful, too."

Sammy had been fighting so hard against Noreen in her mind, but now that they were in here together she could see why the woman was disappointed. The efforts that'd been made on the house over the years were purely for whatever was cheap at the moment without any concern over the integrity of the house. She suddenly felt incredibly guilty for not wanting this house to be worthy of the preservation list.

"What about the light fixture?" she asked, pointing up at the chandelier.

Noreen waved her hand dismissively. "A cheap knockoff, something meant to look fancy that isn't anything more than glass." She stomped off into the library.

By the time the two of them had made it around the lower level, Noreen had done a lot more sighing and shaking her head than anything, and Sammy noticed she'd hardly taken any pictures.

“Maybe there will be something of interest upstairs,” Sammy said brightly.

“Yeah. We’ll see.” Noreen led the way, pointing out the servants’ staircase at the back of the kitchen.

Sammy didn’t hear any raccoons or slamming doors, but she had to admit to herself she was listening for them. She’d gotten past trying to convince Noreen not to worry about the house, even though a spooky encounter could be just the trick to send the Historical Society running. Or would that make them run toward the house even faster? Sammy couldn’t be sure.

On the third floor, Noreen deemed the staircase to the tower unfit for use, and they returned to the entryway. She stood for a long minute making notes on her clipboard until she finally snapped her head back up to look at Sammy. “I’ll present all my information to the Historical Society at our monthly meeting. I’ll also look over any documented history we have on file for the house and add it as well.”

“How long until I know?” Sammy asked, wishing she could at least get started on sweeping and dusting. The house wasn’t theirs, and the sale process hadn’t even truly begun, but she was itching to do something productive.

"I can't make any promises, so I won't try," came Noreen's brusque reply. "In the meantime, I wouldn't do so much as hang a curtain. Thank you for showing me around." She barreled out the door and to her car before Sammy had the chance to be polite and say goodbye.

Sammy made sure all the lights were turned off, leaving on only the porch light so she could see to lock the door. It also just seemed like a safe thing to do, and maybe if the neighbors thought someone lived there they wouldn't keep spreading rumors about it being haunted. She smiled to herself as she imagined some poor woman from down the street knocking on the door with a casserole in hand. As Sammy drove home, she wasn't sure what she hoped Noreen would say once they'd had their meeting.

6
UNEXPECTED GUESTS

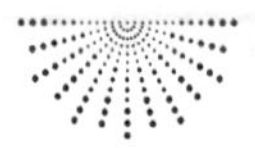

It had been a week since she'd walked Noreen through the house. Sammy hadn't been sleeping well, and she was starting to think her work was suffering. She was tired all the time, and her cakes and cookies didn't seem quite as good as they used to.

"You're dead on your feet," Kate pointed out. "You need to find some way to relax."

"I don't think I can. I'm obsessed," Sammy admitted, swiping a strand of her curly blonde hair behind her ear as she headed into the kitchen. "I want this so desperately, but I'm really torn. If the house needs to be put on the preservation list, then that can only be a good thing for the town. Of course, it also means I have to find some other place to put the shelter."

"Don't get yourself down. Even if you can't use this house, you could always have someone else give you a bid on putting up a building. Like one of those metal pole barns. Those are pretty cheap."

"I've looked into those, actually," Sammy admitted. "I told Rob about it, and he said they're not allowed within city limits. A shelter in the middle of the country won't do those folks any good."

Kate snapped her fingers in disappointment. "I hadn't thought of that."

"In a way, I'm kind of glad. A metal building has the potential for being cheaper, but it doesn't look as homey. I know they'll just be glad to have a roof over their heads no matter what it looks like, but I think the idea of something a little cozier is nice. It's like they're staying at a friend's house instead of just being put up in some sort of barracks."

Kate smiled. "That's exactly why you're the perfect person for the job. Now go home and get some rest before all your enthusiasm kills you."

"Actually, I'm going to stay here for a bit. I promised Helen I'd get ahead on the breakfast baking, so I've got a lot of cinnamon rolls and biscuits to make. We should have quite a demand for them over the weekend." The patrons who came in too late on the previous weekend had experienced the disappointment of finding out Just Like Grandma's was fresh out of their favorites.

"Then let me stay and help you." Kate had just finished untying her apron, but she wrapped the strings back around her waist.

"You don't have to do that," Sammy countered. "You've had to make up enough time for all my absences from work. I've got to be a responsible adult here. Just because there are other things I want to do doesn't mean I don't have to keep up with my obligations."

"Many hands make light work," Kate insisted as she tightened the bow behind her back. "Besides, my Aunt Georgia is in town and I'd love an excuse not to go have yet another dinner with her and my mother. All I'll hear about is how I'm not married yet. Just tell me what to do."

In the end, even though she felt a bit guilty, Sammy was very grateful for Kate's help. The work was much more enjoyable when she had someone there to talk to, and by the time they left there was more than enough baking done to get a good start on the weekend.

"I almost miss living upstairs," Sammy admitted. "It made for a really short commute, and that was lovely on nights like this." The apartment over the restaurant had suffered from frozen pipes in the dead of winter. That had all been fixed now, but Sammy had purchased her own home on Poplar Street.

"Has Helen said anything about what she's going to do with it now that it's empty?" Kate asked, putting the flour canister away.

"Not to me. I'll have to remember to ask her tomorrow. Have a great evening!" Sammy walked out back to her Toyota. She was tired, and she knew she needed to get home. She needed time to unwind before she attempted going to bed, maybe with some mindless television. But her hands guided the wheel over to Liberty Street for just one more look at the house.

She expected to see a quiet, stately house in the older neighborhood, where gaps in the asphalt revealed the original brick street. She thought there might be someone out for a late jog, perhaps a few kids on their bikes trying to get home before the streetlights came on, and maybe a couple of neighbors chatting over a fence.

There was none of that, but what she did see froze her heart in her chest. Sammy knew she'd left the porch light on, but there were other lights shining out through the windows of the house. They danced back and forth frantically, small beams of bright light that definitely weren't coming from the aged light fixtures in the house.

Part of her wanted to pull in the driveway and charge inside, but Sammy knew that wasn't the right way to go about this. She continued for half a block down the road before pulling up to the curb and turning the car around to face the house. She grabbed her phone and quickly dialed the familiar number.

"Jones here."

"It's Sammy. I think someone's broken into the house."

"Into your house? Are you in the home right now?"

She shook her head, even though he couldn't see her. "No, not my house. The one on Liberty Street. I can see flashlights through the window."

"I see." There was some scuffling on his end of the phone for a second. "I'm on my way. Where are you?"

"Parked a little bit down the street."

He hesitated, as though he was trying to decide something. "All right. You stay right there and keep an eye on them, but don't do anything. Don't try to get into the house, and if they leave don't follow them."

"But—"

"Don't argue with me, Sammy. You know I let you play fast and loose a lot more than I should, considering you're not on the force. As a matter of fact, I need to hire you one of these days just so I can issue you a formal reprimand. But we don't know who's in the house or why, and it's better if you just hang tight. I'll be right there. I promise." Jones hung up.

Sammy didn't know if she should be angry or relieved. She didn't really want to go in the house by herself and confront the trespassers, but once he'd told her not to, it was what she wanted more than anything to do. She shook her head, knowing she was thinking like a toddler who was told they couldn't have a second piece of chocolate cake.

Instead, she waited as patiently as she could. It was difficult as she watched those flashlights move through the house. Initially, they'd been in the dining room. Now, they made their way steadily upwards, exploring the second floor and then the third. Sammy imagined those raccoons making some interesting noises to scare them. When she saw the lights finally make their way up to the top of the tower, she was simply angry.

Jones pulled up, his squad car silent as he parked along the curb on the opposite side of the road. The flashlights were coming back down, so the timing was good. He moved toward the house and disappeared into the shadows.

Sammy tapped her fingers on the steering wheel and bit her lip, waiting. She imagined Jones finding his way into the house, and she hoped that whoever had broken in wasn't dangerous. Anyone in law enforcement knew they were putting their lives on the line, but truly threatening events didn't happen often in Sunny Cove. Sammy sent a silent prayer up that everything would work out all right.

Soon enough, the flashlights went off and the overhead lights in the house came on. Sammy traced the progress of the sheriff as he flipped lights on heading down into the main hall, and she couldn't take it anymore. She got out of her car and met him in the front yard just as he came out the door.

Two young men trailed along behind him, looking ashamed and scared. One had a dark fringe of hair that hung down over his eyes from underneath his knit cap. The other had blonde hair and a smug look on his face.

Jones gave her a hard look when he saw her. "Turns out we've got a couple of wannabe ghost hunters on our hands."

"We're not wannabes," the blonde one insisted. "We do this all the time, and we're good. You should see how many followers we have online. Phantom Films is so popular, we're probably going to get some sort of contract with one of the streaming companies."

"Shut up," the dark-headed one commanded. "Nobody's going to give us anything with my leg like this." It was only when he mentioned it that Sammy noticed he was limping. The leg of his pants was torn, and blood was dripping down into the top of his shoe.

"Are you kidding?" the blonde replied. "You got injured by a ghost. That's going to pay off for us, big time."

"What happened?" Sammy knew a ghost couldn't have done this, but she was curious about their side of the story. Jones was busy talking into his radio, so she had a minute.

"It pushed me down the stairs," the boy insisted. "We were already picking up on tons of paranormal activity in the house, and then this. It's going to be great."

"There aren't any ghosts in there," Sammy insisted. "And you had no right to be on this property."

"Oh. Are you the owner?" The smug blonde boy suddenly looked a little less superior.

"The owner lives out of the state," Jones replied for her. "I'll have to get in contact to see if he wants to press charges. In the meantime, I've got an ambulance on the way for you." He gestured at the injured one.

"And what about me?" the fair-headed one asked meekly.

"You're coming down to the station while we sort this whole thing out. The two of you sit down right there and wait patiently." He pointed his finger to the bottom step of the porch, where both of the boys immediately slumped like scolded children.

Sammy almost felt bad for them until she remembered they were the ones who'd broken the law.

The sheriff took her by the arm and led her a few steps away. "As far as I can tell, they were genuinely in there just to make a video. The only damage they did was to break the lock on the back door, and I think we can let them go as long as they pay for that."

"What about his leg?" Sammy looked around Jones to where the young man was peeling back the ripped denim of his pants and examining the injury. "What happened there?"

The sheriff gave a shrug. "I don't really know, but there are plenty of possibilities when you're trespassing on abandoned property. He hurt himself by being stupid, and he's going to blame it on a ghost just to get publicity."

"I don't like this," Sammy admitted. "Everyone is determined to say there are ghosts here. It doesn't make sense."

His intense blue eyes were on hers. "People are naturally afraid of old and abandoned places, just like they're afraid of the dark. It doesn't have to make sense. It just is."

"And now it might affect what I'm going to do with this shelter." What a shame it would be to throw all that time down the drain. At the rate things were going, she wouldn't have a shelter ready to go for another year.

"That part's up to you. But don't let a couple of dumb kids affect your decision. If they really have been doing this little show of theirs for a while, then that means they've gone to lots of ramshackle places in the vain hope of finding a ghost. I would think, though, that if they'd found anything legitimate, we all would've heard about it by now."

"Good point." Sheriff Jones was always after the practical angle, and Sammy found that sometimes she needed to hear it.

"Here comes the ambulance. I'll keep you posted. You'd better get home and get some rest." The flashing lights from the top of the emergency vehicle shone on his face, highlighting the concern there.

"I will. And thanks." Sammy turned and walked back down the sidewalk toward her car, shaking her head.

7

PHANTOM FILMS

It was only a short drive back to her place, but it felt like it was taking forever. Sammy was simply exhausted. As she walked in her front door, she wondered how she was even going to manage making dinner for herself.

The knock on the front door startled her, but Sammy was relieved to find Chelsea standing on the threshold. "Hey! Whoa, hey. Are you all right? Are we still on for dinner tonight?"

Sammy slapped her hand to her forehead and held it there. "I completely forgot. Everything's been so crazy lately. Come on in."

"Have you at least eaten?"

Her stomach growled in response.

"I'll take that as a no. Why don't we order some delivery? Or I can run down the street and hit the drive-thru at Hamburger Hideaway?"

Sammy enjoyed the home-cooked food at Just Like Grandma's, and when she wasn't at work she often took the time to cook for herself. But there was something about a greasy burger out of a paper bag that just sounded amazing. "If you fly, I'll buy."

Fifteen minutes later, when they were seated at the couch with their burgers, Sammy told her about the events of the evening. "I know I shouldn't let it bother me. They're just a couple of kids, and everyone is trying to use the internet to make a buck these days. But what I want to know is how they found this particular house? Sunny Cove is in the middle of nowhere. The only people who've heard about it are the ones who were born here."

Chelsea picked up a fry between two perfectly manicured nails and studied the salt on its surface. "For the most part, sure. But I imagine it's a little different in the ghost-hunting community. They're not looking for places that are popular or well-known. They just want places that will give them some good results."

"Or no results, in the case of that house. I've been in the place three times now, and I can promise you there aren't any ghosts there."

"That you've seen anyway," Chelsea teased. "Maybe the ghosts like you, and that's why they don't bother you."

Sammy tipped her head. "You don't believe in this stuff, do you?"

"No, but I do think the shows are fun. I used to watch spooky stuff on TV all the time with my dad. My mom hated it, but it was like our secret guilty pleasure. I still watch it when I get the chance, and now there are quite a few teams that post their videos online."

That gave Sammy an interesting idea. "These kids said their videos were really popular. I bet they have something online we can go check out." It probably wouldn't help her understand why everyone in the world was trying to scare her away from this house.

"Absolutely! Did they say what their handle was?"

Sammy took out her laptop, trying to think. "Phantom Films, or something like that."

"Oh!" Chelsea clapped her hands. "I've watched some of their stuff before. They're not as good as some of the others. I really like the ghost hunting videos where they use electronics to try to pick up on voices and temperature changes and things like that. These kids just walk through and scare themselves, but it's still fun." She helped Sammy find the right channel on a popular video platform.

Sure enough, the most recent video that had been uploaded featured the two boys standing in front of the house on Liberty Street. She hit the play button.

"Hey, everyone! You know I'm Jordan, and this is Tommy, and tonight we're going to bring you one of the best haunted house tours yet." The camera switched from showing the boys to angling up at the house.

"This place just *looks* haunted," said the blonde one, who Sammy now knew to be Tommy, while the camera panned over the peeling siding, the boarded windows, and the numerous cobwebs in the eaves. "So creepy. Guaranteed we're going to see some activity here."

The video turned back to Jordan. "Now folks, this time we're not going to reveal our location until we've completed this inspection, since there are some out there who like to swipe our sites out from under us." He pointed at the lens. "You know who you are."

Now Tommy's face took up the screen again. "Legend has it that Mary Elizabeth Johnston was born in this house in 1885. She died a mysterious death in 1900, when she was only fifteen years old. Nobody knew exactly what happened, and nobody would admit it, but some in the town suspected she was murdered by her older sister. Her parents buried the girl in the backyard to help cover it all up."

"And now," Jordan continued, "the ghost of Mary Elizabeth is reported to still travel through this home at night. Neighbors have seen her in the windows at night, and one witness said she even stepped out onto the lawn. Nobody has lived here in over a decade, and I think we know why."

"But check back later tonight, and we'll have all the details for you!" Tommy enthused. "Watch our latest release, if you dare!" He wiggled his fingers at the screen, and then it went blank.

"Wait, that was it?"

"Yep, just a teaser. They do that a lot just to build up the hype about wherever they're going next." Chelsea scrolled through some of the other videos.

"Have you ever heard of that young woman they mentioned? Mary Elizabeth Johnston?" Sammy had spent most of her adult life away from Sunny Cove, but an old ghost story like that sounded like something she should've known about.

Chelsea turned her gaze up to the ceiling. "I don't think so. Sounds pretty creepy, though, huh?"

"Yeah." Sammy's mind immediately went back to the overgrown area in the backyard of the home, where Noreen had claimed there was probably a cemetery. Was this young woman buried there? Even if she was, would her headstone still be there? She didn't want to disturb the dead to find out, but she was very curious.

Her friend, meanwhile, was still interested in the Phantom Films channel. "Oh, here. Check this one out."

In this recording, Jordan and Tommy were in what looked to be an abandoned office building. They spent the next ten minutes of footage exclaiming that they heard bumps and footsteps, but Sammy didn't pick up on any of it.

"It's really just for fun," Chelsea explained. "I've watched far more of these than I'd like to admit, and it's not like there's ever any conclusive evidence."

Sammy was looking for evidence, but not evidence of ghosts. "What did they mean when they said others were trying to steal their locations?"

"Oh, it's this big rivalry that's started between Phantom Films and Ghosts, Incorporated. I honestly think the feud is just another way of getting attention for both channels." Chelsea tapped away on the keyboard and pulled up a different team of paranormal investigators. "These guys are more professional. They do the technical stuff like I was talking about before, with EVP and infrared and things like that."

"If they're doing so much more, then why don't they like Jordan and Tommy?" The boys had certainly ruined her evening, but in the end it seemed like they were just harmless kids.

Chelsea lifted a hand in the air. "I don't know. You'd think there are plenty of spooky places in this country to go around. Oh, but look at this." She clicked on a video entitled, "How Phantom Films is Tricking You."

Two grown men stood outside in the night. "Folks, we need to talk a little bit about another channel that a lot of people have been watching and subscribing too. I wouldn't normally name names, but Phantom

Films is nothing but a hoax. They're falsifying information to make houses *seem* haunted, just so they'll have material for their show." This line of thought continued on for a while as the men tried to prove their points, slandering the younger ghost hunters.

Sammy sat back, thinking. "Interesting stuff. I wonder why these guys are so interested in pointing out the flaws of Jordan and Tommy. I mean, it's all fake."

"You've got me. Maybe Sheriff Jones will let you talk to them and you can find out more."

"Maybe. It didn't sound like he could hold them for very long." Sammy picked at her fries, no longer interested in watching these paranormal shows that boasted evidence of the supernatural even when it clearly wasn't there. She only wanted to know the truth, and that seemed harder and harder to find the more she looked.

8
A LITTLE RESEARCH

"Thank you so much for meeting me here," Sammy said breathlessly when she found Viola at the Sunny Cove Public Library the next afternoon. "I hate to admit that I have no idea what I'm doing."

"Not a problem at all!" Viola Hampshire was a member of the Radical Grandmas, a small group of older women who were always on the lookout for some way to benefit the community. With her short gray hair and hawklike nose, Viola reminded Sammy of Dorothy from *The Golden Girls*. She'd worked at the library for a very long time, so Sammy knew she was the perfect person to ask for help. "Actually," the older woman said, "I'm not surprised you needed help looking up old records. Nobody uses the library for research anymore, not like they used to in the old days."

"Well, it was the only place I could think to go that might actually have the answers I'm looking for." Sammy pulled a notebook out of her bag, along with several pens. "I need to find the birth and death records for someone who lived over a hundred years ago. I checked online on some of the genealogy sites, but I didn't have much luck."

Viola nodded with understanding. "That's the problem, you know. Everybody wants to go to the computers for the answers. Personally, I think there's something much more special about actually looking things up in books, in card catalogs, and in old files. I think people retain it better than they do when they just type it in and read it on a screen. I found an article about that once that I'll have to copy and send to you when I think about it. Now then, tell me about this person you're trying to find. Is it a relative of yours?"

"Not exactly." Sammy hesitated for a moment, glancing around to make sure they were the only ones in their section of the library. There was no telling just how many people in Sunny Cove might've seen the Phantom Films teaser video about the 'haunted' house on Liberty Street. Personally, she hoped it was nobody but herself and Chelsea. She didn't want the word to spread any further until she could get to the bottom of it. "You see, I'm trying to buy this house to use as a homeless shelter—"

"Yes, the haunted Victorian on Liberty. So I've heard. It could really be a beautiful place if you got it fixed up. It's a shame someone came through and put all that nasty carpet in there. I mean, it was the style of the times and everything, but still."

Sammy thought her jaw might hit the table. "You already knew? And how did you know about the inside of the house?"

The older woman smiled. "One of my best friends grew up there, Sue Ellen Johnston. I used to go to her house to play all the time. Now, the only thing I really noticed about the place as a girl was how big it was compared to our tiny little house down the street, but as an adult I have to wonder why someone would remodel it the way they did." She clucked her tongue as she looked off in the distance, no doubt traipsing down memory lane.

The hairs on the back of Sammy's neck stood up. "Johnston? Did you say her name was Johnston?"

"Oh, yes. I think she married a Hobart."

The air had left Sammy's lungs, but she forced it back in. She needed help, and Viola was even more of the perfect person to help her than she'd realized. "Did Sue Ellen ever say anything about a girl that died in the house around 1900? You see, this pair of ghost hunters claims there was a girl by the name of Mary Ellen Johnston and that her ghost still haunts the place. When I was at the house to do a walkthrough with the lady from the Historical Society, I found an overgrown area that she said could be a cemetery. I'm trying to find out the truth before I go stepping on anyone's graves."

Viola flourished her fingers in the air. "A real-life mystery! My favorite! You know, I read every single book that was in the mystery section when I worked here. I'm sure they've added more since then, and these old eyes can't take in all the words like they used to, but I still love a puzzle. Now, let's see." She tapped her finger on her chin. "I can't recall Sue Ellen saying anything along those lines. Of course, her mother never would've tolerated it. She was very strict. Ha, if anything, it was Sue Ellen's mother who haunted that house. She never left it except to go to church, and she was the last one to live in it. As you can see, nobody was interested in buying it after she died."

"Do you think we could find the records for this Mary Elizabeth?" Sammy pressed. She was eager to get down to the details. The sooner she knew whether this mysterious dead woman had truly existed or not, the better.

"I'm sure we can. Come with me." Viola led Sammy into a room at the back of the building. It smelled of old paper and musty carpet, and nobody else was there. In fact, Viola had to turn on the light. "All the old public records were transferred here from the courthouse once they started going with a computer system. The clerks didn't want to keep up with it anymore, but the library was happy to. Do you have a date of birth?"

Sammy shrugged. "Supposedly 1885. But I don't have a month or a day."

"How about the death?"

"1900, and nothing else."

"All right, then it'll be a little bit of a hunt, but there's nothing wrong with that. Viola pulled out one drawer of files. "You start here on the birth records, and I'll go look in the death records. With a little bit of luck, we'll find something."

The two of them worked for an hour with no luck.

"I'm so sorry I've wasted your time," Sammy said genuinely. "I should've known it wasn't real."

But Viola wagged her finger in the air. "Tut, tut! It wasn't a waste of time at all! Our little town doesn't have the money to digitize these old records, and I for one am glad. It's a nice little bit of nostalgia to see papers that were actually filled in with a typewriter. It was fun, and we're not by any means done."

"We're not?" Sammy had assumed that a lack of information meant her suspicious about Jordan and Tommy were correct. They'd made the whole thing up just to have good material for their show.

"Oh, no. You forget that we still have the Historical Society to explore."

Sammy made a face. "I don't know if I want to go there. Noreen Heinz didn't seem very pleased with me when she found out what I wanted to do with the house, and she hasn't called me back to give me an update. I'm worried what the verdict will be."

But Viola had the wisdom, patience, and self-confidence of the elderly. "I'm not worried about what they think, and you shouldn't be either. Even if Noreen is there herself!"

"If the records for Mary Elizabeth aren't here, then why would they be there?" Sammy questioned.

"You might be surprised what they have," Viola said patiently. "There should at least be some information on the house, and anything they've found that's tied to it. That could include this Mary Elizabeth. If nothing else, it'll be interesting. Their archives go way back to the beginning of Sunny Cove."

Sammy swallowed. She knew she shouldn't be afraid of Noreen. Everyone else was worried about ghosts, but she was worried about an old woman who didn't like her. "Okay. Let's go."

The Sunny Cove Historical Society was located in a brick house on the south side of town. It didn't look any different from the other homes around it except for the sign out front. A small plaque near the front door denoted the home as belonging to the sister-in-law of some war hero that Sammy vaguely remembered learning about in school.

A volunteer greeted them at the front desk inside what used to be a living room. "Hello, ladies! Is there anything I can help you with today?"

"We're just here to look up some information on a house," Viola explained.

The volunteer gestured through another doorway. "Are you familiar with our archives? Would you like some assistance?"

"We can handle it," Viola assured her as she stepped into the next room.

Sammy was more than grateful to have someone so knowledgeable on her side. Viola seemed perfectly comfortable in the room full of filing cabinets that greatly resembled the room at the library. "Did you spend a lot of time here when you still worked at the library?" she asked, marveling over a picture of the original courthouse that hung on the wall.

"All the time," Viola replied, a happy tone to her voice. "There was nothing I liked better than when someone came to the library needing help finding information. These days the librarians are just like everyone else. They punch the title of a book into the computer, and it tells them exactly where to find it. But you know, when I first started at the library, folks would call in with actual questions. If we didn't know the answers, we'd write the question down, look up the information, and call the customer back."

"Wow. That's a lot of work," Sammy marveled.

"Oh, yes, but I loved it. The internet stopped most of that, and unfortunately not everyone gets the right information these days. Well, anyway. I should stop reminiscing about old times and get onto the matter at hand, shouldn't I?" Viola stepped up to a series of long thin drawers. "These are maps of the city, organized by year. Do you have any idea how old the house is?"

"As far as I know, it was 1885." Sammy watched with awe as Viola quickly flipped through the maps to find the one she needed.

She pulled the drawer all the way out, creating a table-like platform, and gestured for Sammy to come take a look. "Now, I could just as easily have pulled out a current plat map, because we know the house is there right now. But I think it's more interesting to see what the neighborhood was like back when the house was built. I believe this is it right here." She tapped her finger on a rectangle of land on Liberty Street.

Sammy nodded. "That's the one. But I don't think there's as much property with it now."

"Oh, exciting! Let's compare it to something more current." Just a few minutes later, they found out that the land the house stood on had indeed shrunk in size. "I know that's probably not relevant to what you need to know, but you have to allow a little bit of amusement to an old researcher. Now then, the parcel number is used as a cross-reference for a file that contains any other information they might have on the house. Let's see what we can find."

The file on the old Victorian wasn't as fat as some of the other ones in the drawers, but it still had quite a bit of information. Sammy was excited to find a few photos, including one from when the house was first built. "Oh, look at that! It was absolutely grand!"

There were a few newspaper clippings related to the owners of the home, but nothing that pertained to any sort of murder. The name of Mary Elizabeth Johnston was nowhere to be found.

"I think that proves it," Viola confirmed. "We can double-check with the newspaper office, but I know the volunteers here are very thorough. If a suspicious death had taken place at that house, then there'd be some sort of proof."

Sammy felt at least some relief. "Now I just have to figure out how to get everyone else to believe it's not haunted. And I have to wait for the executive board to make a decision on the house. I feel like I'm hanging from a tightwire every day, waiting for a phone call."

Viola looked thoughtful. "Let's take these to the front desk and request some copies." She piled everything back in the folder and brought it to the same young woman who'd greeted them when they arrived. "We'd like a copy of the entire folder, please."

The volunteer was unfazed. "Not a problem. Did you want archival quality? We can do some excellent reprints of the photos for only a little bit more money."

"That would be lovely, dear. Now, can you tell me when the executive board is set to meet next? There are some issues they'll be discussing that I'm curious about." She smiled amiably.

"Let's see." The woman checked a calendar on her desk. "Looks like they just met last week, so it'll be almost another month."

Viola cast a knowing look over her shoulder at Sammy. "That's interesting."

Sammy took that as her cue to step forward. She didn't imagine that she could ever be as confident and charismatic as this Radical Grandma, but she could at least try. She tapped a finger on the folder. "I was supposed to hear back from Ms. Heinz about the status of this house. I'm interested in buying and renovating it, and she said the board would have to make the final decision on my plans."

"And nobody has notified you?"

Sammy shook her head.

The volunteer made a sour face. "That's strange. Give me just a second to look through the notes from the meeting." She sat down at her computer and clicked a few buttons before smiling brightly at Sammy. "The board couldn't find any real historical significance, and most of the original interior of the home has already been changed out. They just ask that you leave the window surrounds intact to maintain the outward appearance, but the house won't actually be on the preservation list."

Sammy couldn't stop the smile on her face. "Now that I can do. Thank you very much." She left her information with the volunteer to retrieve her copy of the file when it was ready, and she and Viola walked out. "I can't thank you enough for all that. I had no idea how interesting it could be to dive into local history like that, even if we didn't find any profound information."

"It can be quite a rabbit hole, I assure you. If there's anything else you need help with dear, you just call me up. I always love a good mystery."

"I'll do that. And your next meal at Just Like Grandma's is on me." Sammy headed for home, feeling like she was finally getting somewhere. She might not be able to stop the rumors about the house, and that might be a battle that would take a long time. But at the very least, she could proceed on the house. She called Rob to give him the good news.

9
A GHOST OF A CHANCE

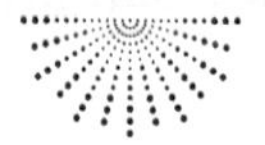

"Hey, Sammy. Are you sitting down?"

Sammy felt herself pale a little as she sank down onto a stool in the kitchen at Just Like Grandma's and pressed her cell phone against her cheek. As soon as she had told Rob the good news about the Historical Society, he promised to get a hold of a home inspector. "I am now."

The attorney heaved a heavy sigh. "Okay, so I took the inspector to the house today."

"Yes?" He was killing her with the suspense. Mr. Lowry had gone over his proposal with them, and they were in budget along with the price of the house. But all of that would go straight down the drain if the foundation wasn't stable or if there were other problems they'd encounter along the way.

"Mr. Furler said we had to keep in mind that this is a really old house. We're going to have to do a lot to make sure the electrical and plumbing are all up to code, especially if we're using it as a shelter and not as a private residence."

"And?" She knew there had to be more, and she was desperate for him to get to the point.

"And," Rob continued, "we are good to go. The inspector said he was actually quite surprised at how little structural damage the house has considering how old it is, and the fact that it was remodeled several times over the years means that we're not trying to deal with hundred-year-old electricity."

"Ah!" Sammy squealed and then covered her mouth, sure that she'd disturbed everyone in the restaurant. "This is amazing! Everything is finally coming together!"

"I think the only other thing we need is to see what Cliff and Judy think of it," Rob reminded her.

"Yes, I didn't want to really get them involved until we knew it would work. I already feel like I've gotten their hopes up and then let them down by taking so long."

"They understand, trust me. If you're available this evening, I can pick them up behind the department store and meet you at the house."

"You bet!" Sammy couldn't even remember if there was something else she was supposed to be doing that evening, but she didn't care. The shelter had taken precedence over everything for the last few months of her life, and that wouldn't change in the span of one evening.

It was difficult to work the rest of the day, knowing that she had so much ahead of her. But as she served the people of her community that she'd gotten to know so well since she'd come back to Sunny Cove, she knew this was all part of the big plan. God knew what she was doing, even when she didn't.

At the end of her shift, she couldn't get out the door fast enough. Sammy ended up behind Rob's sedan as she headed down Main Street, and she could see that he'd already picked up Cliff and Judy. They were the unofficial leaders of the homeless community, and Sammy couldn't wait to see what they thought. She wanted nothing more than for them to be happy, and she hoped they'd approve.

But when the two cars turned into the driveway in front of the faded yellow house, Sammy felt all her hopes shatter. Every light was on in the big house, the yellow glow coming through the remaining windows and shining through the cracks on the boarded-over ones.

Sammy pulled up next to Rob in the driveway and got out. "Please tell me you were already here earlier."

But he shook his head, looking grimly up at the lit house. "Can't say that I was."

"Who could be in there?" Cliff mused.

"I don't know, but if those boys are back I'll have to tell Sheriff Jones to press charges this time." However, she knew from her previous experience with the young men that they were creeping through with flashlights, not turning on every lightbulb in the house.

Rob had his cell phone out of his pocket. "I'll call it in. There's definitely something fishy here."

But just as he was about to start dialing, a ghostly gray figure appeared in the window of the tower, where the study was. Her hair was piled up on her head in a Victorian fashion, and her dress was made of long, gauzy fabric. She pointed one finger at

Sammy before turning around and moving away from the window.

Sammy knew she should be scared. This was exactly the kind of thing that Phantom Films was looking for and had predicted would happen. But it only enraged her. This was supposed to be a safe place for people who needed shelter, not a fun house! Sammy charged toward the door.

"Sammy? What are you doing?" Rob was following her across the lawn.

"I'm going in there, and I'm going to get to the bottom of this!" Her hands shook a little as she retrieved the key she'd picked up at the realtor's office earlier in the day.

"But we don't know who that is," Rob protested.

"It's not a ghost," Sammy pointed out. It certainly looked like one, but she reminded herself once again that she didn't believe in ghosts.

"Exactly. And that means that it could be anyone. Let me get Sheriff Jones out here, and he'll figure it out." He tugged on her sleeve, trying to get her to come back to the parked cars.

"He's right," Cliff offered. "I've been to a lot of creepy places, but there's no point in you getting hurt."

"That's very kind, but I'm going in. Go ahead and call the sheriff, and you can even tell him what I'm doing. He'll be mad at me, but he'll get over it." She charged into the foyer.

"Then I'm coming with you," Rob determined. He turned around and handed his cell to Cliff. "Call Jones for me, okay? Sammy, wait up!"

Sammy was standing in the entryway. It looked so old and sallow under the yellow lights, with its filthy carpet and peeling wallpaper. On her other visits, Sammy had been able to see the charm and potential in the place. Right now, she just wanted to find whoever was trying so hard to stop her from getting this project done.

"Hello?" she called out into the emptiness. "I know you're here. Just come down and we can talk about it." She peeked into the dining room on one side and gestured for Rob to look in the parlor.

"I don't see anything here," he whispered.

Sammy nodded and then charged up the stairs. "I didn't press charges against Jordan and Tommy. I can be very generous when I want to be, but this is really starting to push my buttons."

Rob scrambled to keep up with her. "What, exactly, is your plan here?"

"I don't really have a *plan*," she admitted. "I just want this to end. I'm not leaving until I figure out who's doing this."

Her friend gave a sigh that turned into a small laugh. "Well, Sammy, nobody can ever say you aren't tenacious. It's exactly why you're the perfect partner. But I'll have to keep reminding myself of that if we encounter a real ghost."

Now it was Sammy's turn to laugh as she stepped off the staircase and onto the landing. "So now it's just a question of who's more stubborn: me or the ghost. Right?"

"Pretty much," he agreed. "I'll go this way."

They split up to examine the rooms on this floor. Here, just like in the rest of the house, every single light was on. They highlighted the condition of the house and the amount of work that lay ahead of her, but that didn't put her off.

"Nothing here," Rob reported when he met her back near the landing. "Third floor?"

She smiled. It was good to know he had her back, even if he hadn't wanted to come in here initially. "I guess this makes us the ghost hunters now, doesn't it?" she joked.

"Here, ghostie, ghostie, ghostie," Rob called in a high-pitched tone as they entered the third-floor hall. "Come out, come out, wherever you are!"

Sammy knew she shouldn't be laughing. This was serious. She was reminded of that when all the lights in the house went immediately off and the two of them were plunged into darkness. Sammy put one hand on the banister and the other on Rob's arm.

"It's all right. You don't have to be scared of the dark," he soothed.

"I'm more scared of falling down all these stairs!" she hissed. "How could all the lights go off at once?"

"It's not a power outage. The streetlights are still on," Rob pointed out.

"The breaker box!" Sammy didn't know a lot about electrical work, but she'd helped her father fix things around the house occasionally. "It's probably in the basement." She took her cell out of her pocket, turned on the flashlight app, and headed back down the stairs.

Rob was behind her as they dashed down the wooden staircase to the second floor, turned, and headed for the first floor. As soon as Sammy's feet hit the ancient flooring, she was on her way to the kitchen, where she remembered there had been a basement door. That was the one place in the house she hadn't been yet, and the idea spooked her a little. But that fright was overcome by her need to find the culprit.

"Careful," Rob whispered over her shoulder as she flung open the basement door. "I came down here with the inspector, and these stairs are rickety."

Sammy clung to the narrow railing anchored into the brick wall as she headed down, shining her makeshift flashlight into the basement. Like the rest of the house, this floor was divided into a long hall down the middle with rooms off to either side. Somehow, that seemed more creepy than one large, open space as most modern unfinished basements had.

"The furnace room is over here." Rob gestured to the right. "That's where the breaker box is."

Sammy tightened her lips as she headed forward, uncertain of exactly what she would find, but then Rob was standing in front of her.

"Let me go first." He took her phone out of her hand.

"I can do it," she argued.

"I know you *can,* but I *should,*" he whispered back emphatically. "Jones will kill me if something happens to you."

She wanted to ask him just what he meant by that, but he turned unto the furnace room. The glow of the phone revealed a room that was essentially empty. Rob crossed to the breaker box, the door of which was still open, and flicked the switches back on. The lights in the basement cast a dim glow, by which Sammy could see that there were still no ghosts here.

"Well, now what?" Rob pondered.

But Sammy looked out into the hall just in time to see the last wisps of a ghostly gray skirt disappearing up the staircase. "There she is!" Sammy bolted out into the hall and toward the stairs. The basement door slammed when she got to the bottom of the stairs. Sammy charged up toward it and shoved it open, looking around the kitchen to see the spectral figure heading up the servants' staircase.

"Sammy, wait!"

But Sammy couldn't wait any longer. She charged up the staircase, surprised at how quickly this thing was moving. She'd already climbed up to the third floor once, and it was clear that she'd have to do the same thing again as the vision continued to spiral upwards. On the third floor, where the servants' stairs ended, the phantom charged out of the attic space and down the hall toward the tower. Sammy's legs were burning from the workout, but she wasn't about to give up.

She could see the ghost fully now, a tall woman with pale skin and that carefully done up hair. Her gossamer dress caught on the banister and ripped as she fled into the tower, and she slammed the door behind her. The shriek that erupted through the house a moment later chilled Sammy's bones, and she swallowed before she opened the door.

There were no lights in the tower, but the light from the hall spilled into the odd little room. The ghost sat on the floor, clutching her leg. The deep gashes that streaked up her calf dripped blood onto the floor.

Sammy looked from the blood to the woman's face. It was caked over with white makeup, but Sammy thought she knew that face. "Noreen?"

"I'm sorry," Noreen said from her seat on the back of the ambulance twenty minutes later. "I've always loved this house, just like I've loved all the other old houses in this town. I'm tired of seeing them razed or remodeled to accommodate modern life."

"I can understand that," Sammy said sympathetically, "but I don't see why you had to cause so much trouble for me. I guess this means there really isn't a cemetery at the back of the property?"

The historian shook her head. "Not at all, or at least not that I know of. It's probably an old herb garden."

Jones leaned against the side of the ambulance. "What about those boys from Phantom Films? Did that have anything to do with you?"

Noreen had wiped most of the white ghost makeup from her eyes, leaving flesh-colored streaks in the middle of her face. She nodded sadly. "There were plenty of rumors about the house, but you already knew that. When Edith told me what you planned on doing with this house, I hoped that would be enough to change your mind. Well, that plus the idea that you might have to work with the Historical Society, which is usually much more work than anybody wants to do. I couldn't get the Society on my side, though, and I've been following Phantom Films online for a while to look for houses that needed help. I hoped they were just what I needed."

"But when you found out we could proceed, you decided to pose as the ghost yourself." Sammy shook her head, surprised that anyone would go to such lengths. But Noreen clearly had a passion for old houses. "I have to give you credit, you're pretty quick."

"I run to keep in shape," Noreen said with a grim smile. "That broken staircase in the tower got me just like it did Jordan. His foot went right through it, and I wasn't thinking about it."

"All right. I think we'd better get you off to the hospital and then down to the station." Sheriff Jones watched as the paramedics loaded Ms. Heinz into the ambulance and then turned to Sammy. "You shouldn't have gone in that house, you know."

"Yeah, I know." She rolled her eyes.

"And I know you were going to go in there anyway, so I'm not surprised. I'm actually more surprised you listened to me the last time when those boys were filming in there. Anyway, I think we've got this all wrapped up unless there are more ghosts you need to round up in there."

Sammy looked up at the house, which was still completely lit up. Once again, she could see all the possibilities in the old structure. “I think we’re good here.”

10

A HISTORIC RECIPE

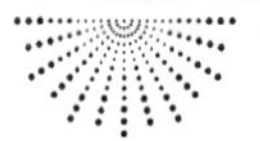

Sammy skimmed her finger down the ancient recipe in the old journal she'd found in the study, so excited to actually be putting these recipes to good use. The handwriting wasn't always easy to read, but it was yet another puzzle for her to work out.

Rob poked his head in the kitchen. "How's everything going in here?"

"Perfect! Let me just put these in the oven and we can take our final walkthrough." Sammy had never made lavender cookies with rose water icing, but they already smelled delicious. "Let's start at the front door. I want to see it just as someone would if they're coming in for the first time."

The two of them went outside, where the sign for Sunny Cove House was placed carefully in the yard. When they walked into the entryway, a stately wooden desk for a volunteer sat off to the side. The windows on the first floor had been replaced, letting in a flood of light as they walked through the common area. While the rooms still served their original functions as kitchen, dining room, living room, and library, the donation from Mr. Montgomery had transformed them into beautiful modern spaces that hinted at the house's original age.

Upstairs, the massive bedrooms had been split into smaller rooms that could accommodate more people and still give them some privacy. In a way, it wasn't too far off from the idea that Andrew Herzog had presented, and he'd even donated electronic locks for each door. Extra bathrooms had been installed, the carpeting had been replaced with wood laminate, and the walls were painted in soft, welcoming colors.

"This is my favorite part," Sammy said as she opened the door to the tower. The lower room wasn't big, but they'd managed to convert it to a break room for volunteers, complete with a small couch, a television, and a coffee pot. Up the stairs at the top of the tower, which had been completely replaced, was an office space for volunteers. They found Noreen at one of the desks.

"Are you ready for the official opening?" Sammy asked brightly.

Noreen looked up over her wireframe glasses and smiled. "I've never been more ready for anything in my life, but there's something I have to tell you first."

Sammy glanced through one of the wide windows that looked out over Sunny Cove, giving a beautiful view of the town. Summer was just around the corner, and the greenery on the trees made everything look fresh and new. "What is it?"

"I just want to thank you." Noreen came around from behind the desk and wrapped her in a hug. "You were so kind to agree to letting me volunteer my services here instead of spending time in jail, and I've enjoyed it much more than I ever thought I would. I thought I would hate seeing this place remodeled, but you've breathed such life into it. It's not like a homeless shelter at all. It's more like a bed and breakfast!"

Sammy beamed, pleased with the assessment. "It's been my pleasure, and we couldn't have done it without you. Now, we'd better get downstairs. I think everyone is about to arrive."

She dashed to the kitchen when they reached the first floor, taking her cookies out of the oven while Rob opened the door. It turned out there were plenty of people interested in seeing the new shelter. Sammy greeted Andrew Herzog and thanked him for donating materials to the project. Chelsea and Heather, who'd put in plenty of time with cleaning gloves and paintbrushes, both wrapped her in hugs. Viola brought the rest of the Radical Grandmas with her to see the lovely display of historic photos in the front entryway. Helen and Johnny arrived carrying large trays of food for the guests. Cliff, Judy, and the rest of their crew couldn't give her and Rob enough praise.

Two young men poked their heads shyly in the door. Sammy recognized their faces and ushered them in. "Jordan! Tommy! Come on in!"

Tommy bit his lip. "We weren't sure you'd want us here. Is the sheriff around?"

"Not yet," Sammy assured them. "But the two of you did a lovely job with the yard. I'm very grateful." The boys hadn't exactly had the money to pay for the damage they did to the back door when they'd broken in, but they did have strong backs.

Jordan shook his head to get his long hair out of his eyes. "I know we already put in our hours, but we had something we wanted to talk to you about before we leave town. I mean, if you have the time."

Sammy could tell they were nervous, and she ushered them into the library. "Of course. What is it?"

"Well, we have a few connections in the online community, you know?" Tommy said, looking at his shoes.

"And we thought there might be something else we could do for you, so we reached out to this other channel. It's called Community Scene, and they specialize in films about projects just like this one. We told them about you, and they'd like to feature this place on their show. With your permission, of course." Jordan twined his fingers together nervously.

"Oh, that's so sweet of you!" Sammy gave them each a hug, grateful that it'd all worked out so well. "Now stop pouting and go get yourselves some food! There's a big buffet set up in the dining room."

She shooed them back to the other side of the house. They skirted widely around the front door, where Sheriff Jones was just walking in.

"Hey, Sammy!" he said with a smile. "Looks like it's really come together."

It'd been two months since she had finally rid the house of its last 'ghosts,' and Sammy had worked her fingers to the bone, but she still felt that same ball of excitement in the pit of her stomach when she thought about everything they'd accomplished. "It really has. I'm so thrilled. I can't tell you how happy I am to know that anyone who needs help can come here. And you won't believe the amount of people who've come forward to volunteer!"

"Sure I do," Jones replied. "I happen to know that every single staff member at the department has pledged some time, myself included."

"Really?" Sammy knew he must've had something to do with that.

"Well, having a safe place for people on the streets means less work for us, actually. The homeless, the runaways, people down on their luck, they can all come here. They don't need to break into someone's garden shed to get out of the rain or scare business owners by diving in the dumpsters."

"Oh, I see. So it's all about work, is it?"

He leveled his gaze at her. "You know it's not. I'm really proud of you, Sammy."

She blushed at the compliment, though she hadn't done it for the praise. Still, it was nice. "Thanks. I'm pretty proud of it all, too."

THANK YOU FOR CHOOSING A PUREREAD BOOK!

We hope you enjoyed the story, and as a way to thank you for choosing PureRead we'd like to send you this free Special Edition Cozy, and other fun reader rewards...

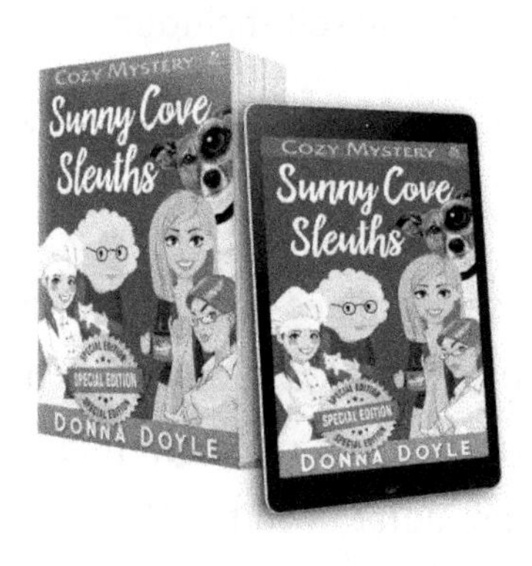

Click Here to download your free Cozy Mystery
PureRead.com/cozy

Thanks again for reading.

See you soon!

OTHER BOOKS IN THIS SERIES

If you loved this story why not continue straight away with other books in the series?

Dying For Cupcakes

Rolling Out a Mystery

Christmas Puds and Killers

Cookies and Condolences

Wedding Cake and a Body by the Lake

A Spoonful of Suspicion

Pie Crumbs & Hit and Run

Blue Ribbon Revenge

Raisin to be Thankful

Auld Lang Crime

Stirring Up Trouble

Haunts & Ham Sandwiches

A Final Slice of Crime

OR READ THE COMPLETE BOXSET!

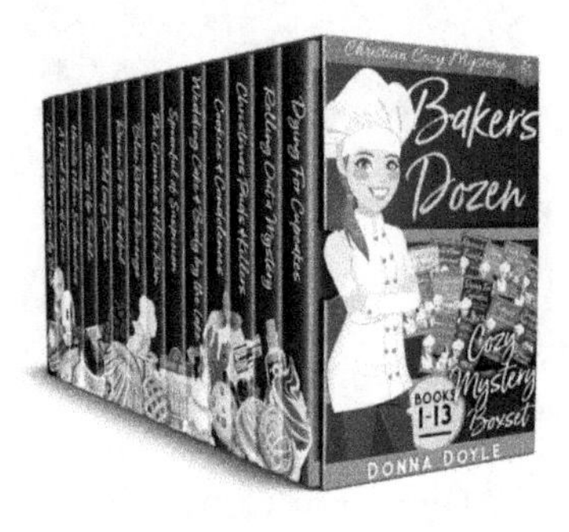

Start Reading On Amazon Now

OUR GIFT TO YOU

AS A WAY TO SAY THANK YOU WE WOULD LOVE TO SEND YOU THIS SPECIAL EDITION COZY MYSTERY FREE OF CHARGE.

Our Reader List is 100% FREE

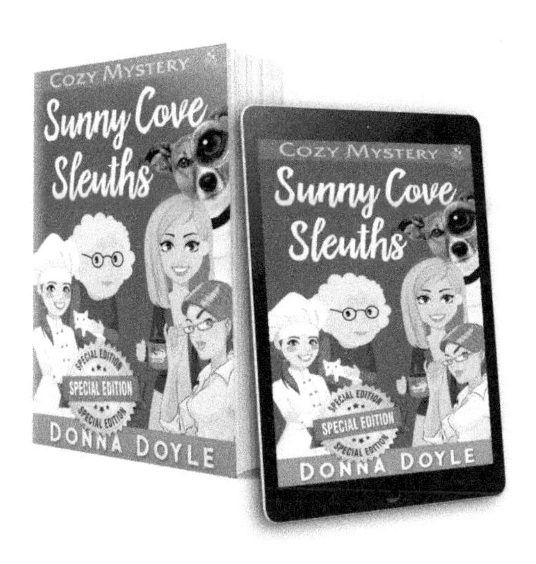

Click Here to download your free Cozy Mystery

PureRead.com/cozy

At PureRead we publish books you can trust. Great tales without smut or swearing, but with all of the mystery and romance you expect from a great story.

Be the first to know when we release new books, take part in our fun competitions, and get surprise free books in your inbox by signing up to our Reader list.

As a thank you you'll receive this exclusive Special Edition Cozy available only to our subscribers...

Click Here to download your free Cozy Mystery
PureRead.com/cozy

Thanks again for reading.
See you soon!

Printed in the USA
CPSIA information can be obtained
at www.ICGtesting.com
LVHW070159090524
779798LV00009B/200